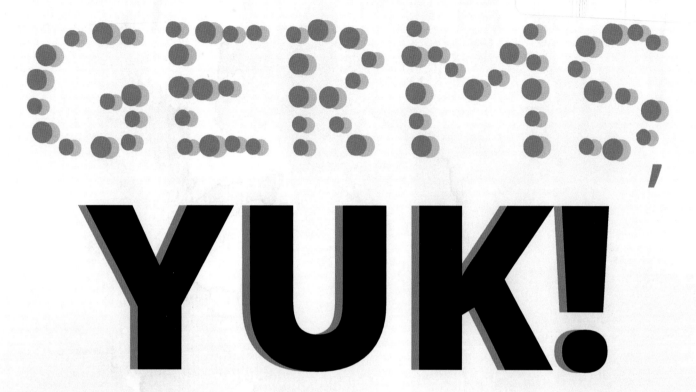

GERMS, YUK!

Little Learners
PUBLISHING

What are   Germs?

Germs are also called Microbes and

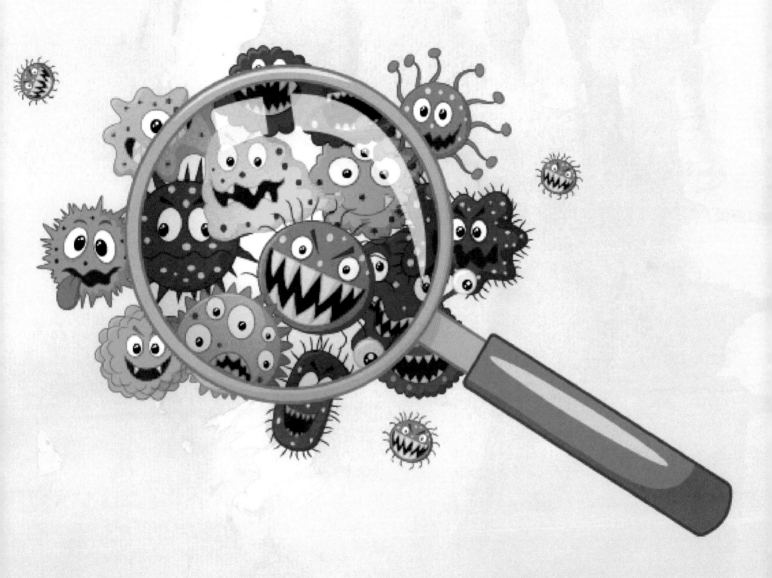

can only be seen under a microscope.

They are

on pets

on doorknobs

on keyboards

on chairs

on bathrooms

on cellphones

on tables

on playgrounds

at restaurants

on money

on your hands

EVERYWHERE!

They can enter your body through your

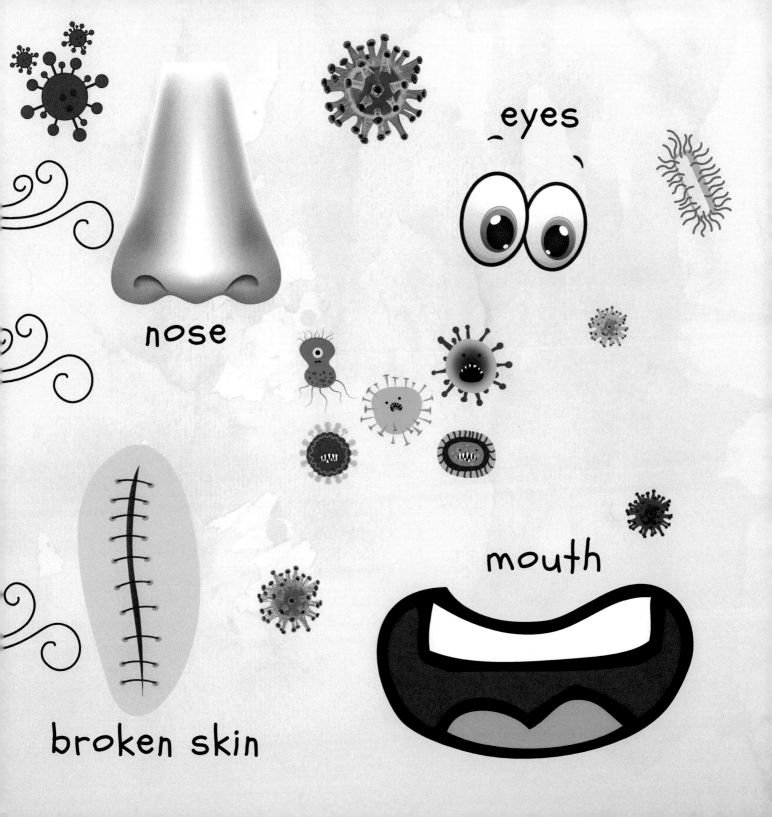

nose

eyes

mouth

broken skin

When they enter your body they multiply

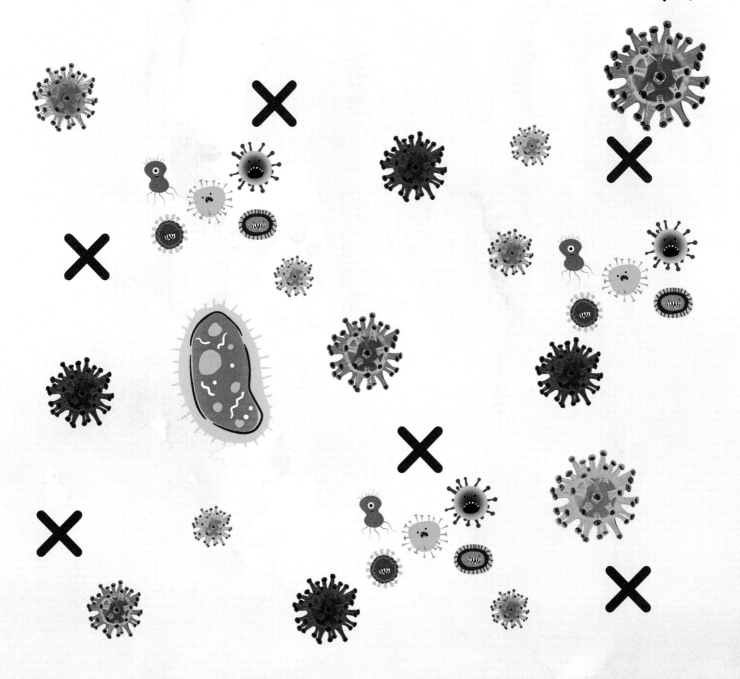

and can start viruses and sickness on

animals

plants

and people.

Then your body has to fight them off

to keep you healthy!

So how do you keep them off?

Soap helps take the germs away!

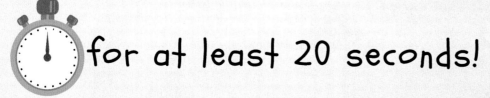 for at least 20 seconds!

Sing your ABCs while washing!

Keep your fingers out of your mouth

Sneeze and cough on your arm

and not on your hands.

Stay home if you are sick

so others don't get sick.

When you blow your nose...

Eat your fruits

and your veggies

Wash your hands before you eat

and after you are done playing

inside

and outside

Cover your Boo-Boos

tumble

flip

fall down

slip

with a bandage so the germs

don't get in your open skin

But most importantly Always

so that we can

STOP
VIRUSES

Manufactured by Amazon.ca
Bolton, ON

14637299R00017